For Finn and George, with love ~ M C B

To my Grandfather Hakon Kristensen ~ T M

This edition published by Scholastic Inc., 557 Broadway; New York, NY 10012,
by arrangement with Little Tiger Press.
SCHOLASTIC and associated logos are trademarks and/or registered
trademarks of Scholastic Inc.
Distributed in Canada by Scholastic Canada Ltd.; Markham, Ontario

First published in the United States by Good Books, Intercourse, PA 17534, 2010

Library of Congress Cataloging-in-Publication Data is available for this title

Original edition published in English by Little Tiger Press,
an imprint of Magi Publications, London, England, 2010

Text copyright © M. Christina Butler 2010
Illustrations copyright © Tina Macnaughton 2010

ISBN: 978-1-84895-074-0

Printed in China

10 9 8 7 6 5 4 3 2 1

One Special Day

M. Christina Butler

Illustrated by Tina Macnaughton

Spring was here at last, and Little
Hedgehog was very excited.
   "The sun is shining, off we go—
      To find out where the bluebells grow!"
he sang, merrily packing his lunch.
   Just then, he heard a voice
calling outside.

It was Ma and Baby Hedgehog.

"Could you look after Baby?" asked Ma anxiously. "I must take care of Mole. He has a terrible cold."

"Oh, my!" replied Little Hedgehog. "Of course!"

"Thank you," she said, giving Baby a big kiss. And off she went.

"We're hunting for bluebells today, Baby!"
smiled Little Hedgehog.

"Whee!" squeaked Baby Hedgehog, as they
set off together. "Baby's hunting bluebells!
And Blankie's coming, too!"

Badger, Fox, and Mouse soon joined them.

"This is my baby cousin," said Little Hedgehog. "He's coming along to help."

"Very nice," nodded Badger, taking the lead.

"A baby?" frowned Fox. "And what's that *thing* he's holding?"

"It's my blankie!" giggled Baby Hedgehog.

"We'll find the best bluebells in Wild Flower
Woods," began Little Hedgehog.

"I see one!" squeaked Baby Hedgehog,
running off into a briar patch.

"Baby! Come back!" cried Little Hedgehog.

"Don't worry; he won't be far away,"
said Badger, as they all began
searching through the brambles.

Suddenly, Baby Hedgehog came out of the bushes, covered in leaves. "For you!" he beamed, holding out a big, blue feather.

"Thank you, Baby . . . but where's your blankie?" said Little Hedgehog.

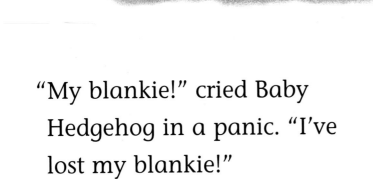

"My blankie!" cried Baby Hedgehog in a panic. "I've lost my blankie!"

"Oh, no!" groaned Fox.

"It's all right, Baby," said Little Hedgehog gently. "We'll find Blankie."

And they began searching the bushes again.

"I've found it!" Mouse's voice came
at last. But as she tugged at the
blanket, suddenly the flower stem
sprung back ... PING!

BUMP!
Mouse fell on her bottom,
and the blanket went sailing
up in the air.

"Blankie, come back!"
squeaked Baby Hedgehog.

Just as the blanket floated to the ground,
Baby Hedgehog dived onto it and went
bumping and bouncing in a blankety ball
down the hillside.

"He'll hurt himself! Stop him!" cried
Little Hedgehog, running after Baby.

"Here we go again," puffed Fox,
racing down the hill.

The blankety ball rolled to a stop, and
Baby tumbled out among the flowers.

"Oh, Baby!" gasped Little Hedgehog.
"Thank goodness you're safe!"
"Baby likes hunting bluebells!"
laughed Baby, as they hugged each other.

"Would you believe it?" smiled Little Hedgehog. "We've reached Wild Flower Woods."

"Ready, set, go!" Badger cried, and off they ran to see who would find the bluebells first.

"Over there!" Mouse shouted out.
"I've found them . . .

EEEEEK!"

"What was that?" exclaimed Fox.

"It was Mouse!" cried Little Hedgehog.
"Come on!"

Mouse had fallen into a deep, dark hole.

"It must be an old rabbit warren,"
muttered Badger.

"Hold on!" called Little Hedgehog.
"We'll get you out."

Little Hedgehog, Badger, and Fox tried and tried, but the hole was just too deep to reach Mouse.

Then Baby Hedgehog got very excited. "Blankie will get Mouse out," he cried.

"That's it!" said Badger. "We'll pull her out with the blanket!"

"Good job, Baby!" said Little Hedgehog proudly.

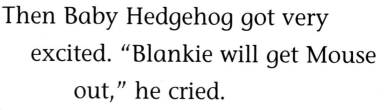

Little Hedgehog and Baby held on
to the blanket tightly, and Mouse
grabbed it.

"One! Two! Three! *Pull!*" cried
Little Hedgehog. Then everyone
tugged, and with one
mighty heave . . .

Mouse popped up out of the hole!

"Hurrah!" they shouted, giggling
and falling back together.

"We found the bluebells," chuckled Badger, "but what a day!"

"And what a hero!" Fox smiled at Baby. "Just like your big cousin, Little Hedgehog."

And chattering and laughing, they all sat down together for a special picnic among the bluebells.